MADDIE
ON A MISSION
Germ Busters to the Rescue

MADDIE ON A MISSION
PUBLISHED BY FROG POND PUBLISHING
P.O. Box 452721
Garland, TX 75045-2721
Paperback ISBN-13: 978-1-7340928-3-7
        ISBN-10: 1-7340928-3-1

Edited by Ann Fields
Published in the United States by Coffee Creek Media Group.

MADDIE
ON A MISSION
Germ Busters to the Rescue

This book is dedicated to:

_____

Today is Monday – school day. Maddie is ready to go back to school after a long spring break weekend.

Maddie skips to the kitchen. **"Good Morning Mommy."**

"I'm so excited. Today I get to see my friends and teachers!" Maddie said.

4

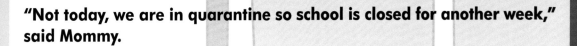

"Not today, we are in quarantine so school is closed for another week," said Mommy.

"Another week?" asked Maddie. **"What is a quarantine?"**

"A quarantine is a time when everyone is asked to stay home so they won't get sick," her mother said. "There is a new virus that is making a lot of people sick. It's called **Coronavirus.**"

5

Maddie's mom shook her head. "Slow down, baby girl! Let me see if I can answer your questions." She began, "A virus is a tiny germ that can pass from person to person, and can make us sick. Sick like when you get a cold, or a sore throat. But much worse."

"Much worse like what Mommy?" asked Maddie.

"Some people may be sick enough to go to the hospital and have to stay for a while. Some people like Grandma and Grandpa whose bodies have a hard time fighting off germs are at greater risk."

7

Maddie listened very closely.

"To stay healthy and strong we all must stay home. That is what quarantine means," her mother said. "We must also wash our hands with soap and water for at least 20 seconds or use hand sanitizer after we have been in any public space, and if we cough, sneeze, or blow our noses. Don't touch your eyes, nose, or mouth with dirty hands," said Mommy.

"If we are sick we should stay at home. If we have to go to the store, we should wear a mask to cover our nose and mouth. We should practice social distancing by staying 6 feet away from others so we won't spread germs."

"Germs are everywhere," Mommy said. "So you must clean things that you touch often. Things like doorknobs, light switches, counter tops, desks, and phones."

"Did I answer everything?" asked Mommy.

Maddie smiled and said, "Yes Mommy you did! **Can I help spread the word?"** asked Maddie.

"Sure Maddie, you can help get the word out," said Mommy.

"I have work to do!" Maddie ran to her room.

She sat down and thought and thought.

"I know!!" Maddie shouted. "I will make my friends Germ Busters!"

To stay healthy and strong you must...

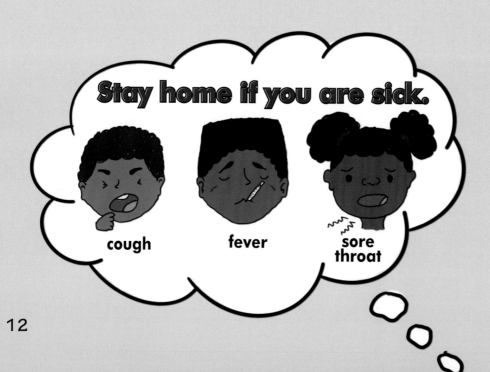

Wash your hands.

After you have been in a public place, use soap and water to wash your hands for at least 20 seconds; the time it takes you to sing the 'Happy Birthday' song.

If you cough, sneeze or blow your nose,

AAA-CHOO!!

don't touch your eyes, nose, or mouth with dirty hands.

Wear a mask.

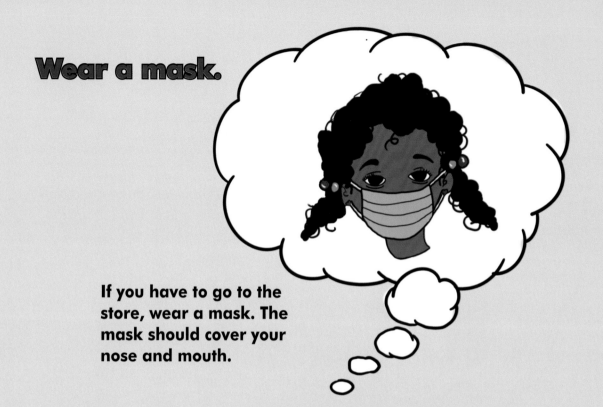

If you have to go to the store, wear a mask. The mask should cover your nose and mouth.

Practice social distancing.

6ft

Stay 6 feet away from others so you won't spread germs.

Germs are everywhere!

So clean things that you touch often.

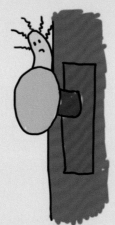

Doorknobs,

ON

OFF

countertops,

desks,

light switches,

and phones.

Maddie created a flier with the information she learned from her mother.

It read:

Become A Germ Buster!
Let's do our part and stop the spread of Coronavirus.

Maddie

She hit the "post" button!

16

Maddie messaged all of her friends asking them to take the pledge to become Germ Busters. One by one, her friends were all sworn in as Germ Busters and shared her post.

Friends of friends, cousins, aunts, uncles, and even teachers shared her post! Before she knew it, her post had gone viral.

She ran to the kitchen, and jumped up and down. "Mommy!" she squealed. **"I did it. I did it!"**

"You did what?" her mommy asked.

"My friends are all sworn in as **Germ Busters** and we spread the word about coronavirus. Mommy, our post went viral!!!"

"Maddie that is wonderful! You guys did a great job. See what happens when we all work together?"

"Mission accomplished!"
said Maddie.

"Mission accomplished!"

20

The End

About the Author/Illustrator

Sharon Jones-Scaife grew up in Marvell, Arkansas, the fourth of 15 children. As one can imagine, she spent a great deal of time reading to her younger siblings. She is a graduate of the University of Arkansas at Little Rock with a BA in Graphic Design and Illustration.

Sharon Jones-Scaife is the publisher of *Teen Graffiti*, a magazine that serves as a voice for teens and as an avenue of communication, allowing teens to express their opinions, concerns, and ideas through poetry, essays, articles, and photography.

Sharon Jones-Scaife is also the author of *I Miss You Papa, Mrs. Hughes is Missing, It's Bedtime Lil' Marco, Lil' Marco Plays Hide and Seek*, and *Becoming*, a collection of original poems and illustrations.

A resident of Sachse, Texas, Sharon Jones-Scaife spends her time supporting her son in basketball, creating adventures with her grandchildren, running, cycling, playing softball, writing, and of course, reading. More information is available at her website at www.coffeecreekmediagroup.com.

About the Author

Dr. Jill Waggoner holds a Medical Degree and a Master's Degree from the University of Oklahoma. She has certifications in both Preventive Medicine and Wellness Coordination from the prestigious Cooper Institute. Dr. Waggoner is a residency trained, board certified Family Practice Physician, with nearly 30 years experience.

She has studied Functional and Integrative medicine for the past 15 years; an approach that seeks to find the cause of disease and uses multiple healing modalities to help patients obtain optimal health. Most recently she received a certification in Plant Based Nutrition from Cornell University. She has dedicated her life to teaching her patients how to flourish and embrace better living through better health. Dr. Waggoner has authored seven books.

She has served as a national medical expert for both television and radio for NBC, ABC and Fox affiliates. Her most rewarding accomplishment is that of wife to her husband Mark, and mother of her two daughters, Jillian and Uriah.

Dr. Jill Waggoner is dedicated to the cause of giving individuals the tools needed to step beyond the traditional approach of early detection of disease, to the futuristic reality of prevention of disease!

You may also like these books by Author Sharon Jones-Scaife!

Your FREE Gift!

FREE Coloring & Activity Book with printables, lesson plans, teacher help, puzzles, mazes, promotions and your child's **Emergency Preparedness Completion Certificate!**

Visit my website to download right now!
www.coffeecreekmediagroup.com
or email contact@coffeecreekmediagroup.com

Follow us online

CoffeeCreekMediaGroup